Gus Makes a Gift

Gus Makes a Gift

by Frank Remkiewicz

Cartwheel
B·O·O·K·S·®

SCHOLASTIC INC.
New York   Toronto   London   Auckland
Sydney   Mexico City   New Delhi   Hong Kong

To Sylvia

Library of Congress Cataloging-in-Publication Data is available.

ISBN 978-0-545-24469-5

12 11 10 9   16/0

Printed in the U.S.A.   40
First printing, April 2011

Gus goes to school.

"Bye, Dad."

Gus loves school.

It is time for art.

What will Gus make?

Gus makes a gift.

Mom will love it.

Here are some beads.

Gus likes beads.

Gus loves red beads.

Gus makes a gift.

"See my beads!" says Tess.

"See MY beads!" says Gus.

"NOW see my beads!" says Tess.

"Now see MY beads!" says Gus.

Oops!

Mom will still love it.

Gus runs home.

Mom loves her gifts.

Happy Mom's Day!